A TOOTHY TONGUE AND ONE LONG FOOT

Nature Activities for Kids

To Casey!
For the worta
to explore in
your back yard.
Happy "investigating".
Love,
Mrs. Roblau
May 8, 1994

A TOOTHY TONGUE AND ONE LONG FOOT

Nature Activities for Kids

Diane Swanson

BOB ADAMS, INC.
Holbrook, Massachusetts

Published by Bob Adams, Inc.
260 Center Street, Holbrook, MA 02343

ISBN: 1-55850-379-X

Printed in the United States of America.

J I H G F E D C B A

This publication is designed to provide accurate and authoritative information with regard to the subject matter covered. It is sold with the
understanding that the publisher is not engaged in rendering legal, accounting, or other professional advice. If legal advice or other expert
assistance is required, the services of a competent professional person should be sought.
— From a *Declaration of Principles* jointly adopted by a Committee of the American Bar Association
and a Committee of Publishers and Associations

Edited by Elaine Jones
Cover and interior design by Warren Clark
Illustrations by Warren Clark and Carolyn Swanson
Typeset by Warren Clark

This book is available at quantity discounts for bulk purchases.
For information, call 1-800-872-5627.

ACKNOWLEDGEMENTS

Many thanks to the following for reviewing sections of this book: Wayne Campbell and Cris Guppy of the Royal British Columbia Museum, Yousuf Ebrahim of the University of Victoria, Bob Louie and Bob Marsh of the B.C. Ministry of Environment, Alison Nicholson of the B.C. Ministry of Forests and private consultant Wayne Swanson. And thanks to Colleen MacMillan and Elaine Jones for guidance.

CONTENTS

NOTE TO KIDS

This book belongs outdoors—with you. Use it to help you explore the natural wonders in your own backyard. You'll surprise your family and friends with the discoveries you'll make. There are few things on Earth stranger than the plants and animals that live close to your home.

Don't worry if you can't name all the insects, birds, plants or rocks you find. It's your observations that count—and all the fun you have making them. So take this book outdoors, and go to it.

NOTE TO PARENTS

This book was written to cultivate a child's sense of wonder in the nature that is close at hand—in her or his own backyard. It was written to encourage children to have fun outdoors all year round.

You do not need to supervise your child in this book's activities. They are designed to lead him or her along easily, step by step. Nor do you or your child need to scrounge around for all sorts of unusual tools. Other than an inexpensive magnifying glass—which your child MUST have to use this book—the activities call only for ordinary household objects.

Your child may want to share her or his discoveries with you. Be receptive. In *A Sense of Wonder*, Rachel Carson wrote, "A child's world is fresh and new and beautiful, full of wonder and excitement." Let your child take you there.

CATERPILLARS TO BUTTERFLIES

Some people believe that butterflies have special powers: they bring good luck, good harvests and good hunting; and they are signs of births, deaths and marriages.

Scientists don't believe that the butterfly has special powers. But it does something that seems quite magical. It hatches from an egg as a long, wingless caterpillar. It grows and sheds its skin several times. Then it hangs upside down and grows a hard skin, becoming a pupa. When it comes out of that skin, it is a beautiful butterfly—a colourful creature that helps spread pollen from flower to flower.

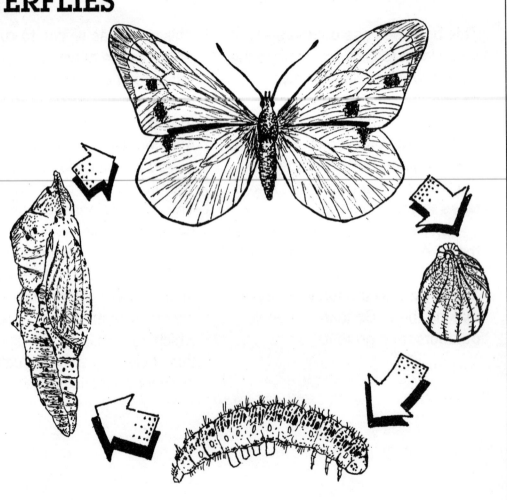

CHECK OUT AN EATING MACHINE

Tools
- Magnifying glass

Steps

1. Find a green, brown or yellowish caterpillar on the leaves of its favourite plant, such as cabbage, broccoli, pansies, red clover or milkweed.

2. Use your magnifying glass to find the caterpillar's eyes. They're tiny and can only see things that are very close.

BIGGEST BUTTERFLIES...AND MORE

- Monarch butterflies fly from Canada to spend winter in Mexico and the southern United States. They fly up to 25 miles per hour, almost as fast as a car travels in the city.
- Biggest butterfly wingspan: about 12 inches, wider than your chest.
- Smallest butterfly wingspan: about half an inch, almost as wide as your thumbnail.
- Caterpillars have more than 4,000 muscles. You have 639.

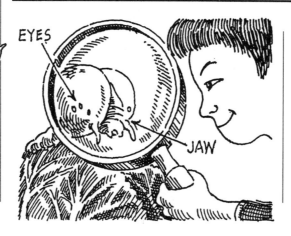

EYES
JAW

3. Notice all the legs under the caterpillar's long body. Only the first 3 pairs are real legs—with joints. When the caterpillar sheds its last skin, it sheds its false legs, too.

4. Watch the caterpillar eat and eat and eat. It feeds most of the time because it's growing very fast. If a caterpillar stopped eating for a day or more, it might die.

5. Notice how the caterpillar is built to eat.

- Its sharp, strong jaws are quick-moving.
- Its short legs keep its jaws close to the leaves.
- Its long body can hold lots of food.

PEEK AT A BUTTERFLY

Steps

1. Stay still near some sweet-smelling flowers. Wait for a butterfly to land on a blossom near you.

2. Watch closely to see how the butterfly feeds. It unrolls its tube-like tongue, then sticks it into a flower and sucks up the nectar.

3. Notice what makes butterflies different from moths: knobs at the ends of the butterfly's feelers. Moths often have feathered or curved feelers.

BUTTERFLY

MOTH

4. Watch for butterflies when you play in your yard. They come in many sizes, colors and designs. See how many different kinds come to your garden. Notice which plants the butterflies like best.

BACKYARD TREASURE

Your yard is full of neat things: rocks hundreds of years old, flowers with "landing strips" for bees, and insects that walk upside down. It's also a likely spot for many birds to feed. The food that some of them eat each day weighs as much as they do.

A treasure hunt is a good way to discover neat things in your backyard. Find the things that are listed below by looking, feeling, smelling and listening. But don't disturb anything. Instead, use a pencil and paper to write down what you find.

HUNT HIGH, HUNT LOW

Tools

- Notepad and pencil

Steps

1. Find each object, sound or smell in the list below—all in the same day. Try it again another day.

- Chewed leaf
- Bee on a flower
- Feather
- Sticky seed
- Sound of moving air
- Water on a leaf

- Black rock
- White cloud
- Animal with 8 legs
- Bud on a twig
- Dandelion leaf
- Flower smell
- Animal home
- Tree smell
- Animal noise

2. Find each object, sound or smell in the list below—all in the same week. Try it again another week.

- Thunder
- Grass smell
- Spider's web
- Bird building a nest
- Insect buzzing
- Animal footprint

- Bent or broken stem
- Rainbow
- Sunrise
- Flower with no smell
- Robin
- Bird song
- A fly upside down
- Speckled stone
- Black cloud

NATURE NOTES

Tsh-ee-EEE E-e-ou

- The sound of a male cicada, a large insect, can travel 440 yards or 1,320 feet.
- A rainbow can last more than 3 hours.
- The smell of sap from a pine tree can clear a stuffy nose.

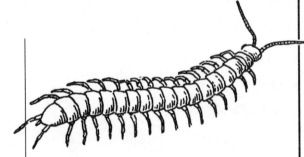

- Some centipedes have more than 300 legs.

FIND A SKINNY/FAT THIS OR THAT

Tools

- Notepad and pencil

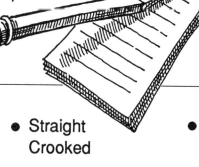

Steps

1. Glance at the list below. It doesn't name anything for you to find. Instead, it lists pairs of words—opposites, like thick and thin—that describe objects, sounds and smells.

- Straight
  Crooked

- Rough
  Smooth

- Light
  Heavy

- Stinky
  Sweet-smelling

- Loud
  Soft

- Tall
  Short

- Black
  White

- Hot
  Cold

- Wet
  Dry

- Strong-smelling
  Faint-smelling

- Sharp
  Dull

- Hard
  Soft

2. Find natural objects that each word in each pair could describe—like a **thick** worm and a **thin** tree. Find them all in the same day.

3. Make up your own list and find the objects on it.

SMOOTH MOVES:
SNAILS AND SLUGS

Slippery snails and slugs slide slowly on silvery slime—in most everyone's yard. Many people don't like these animals because they eat garden plants. But they also help a garden by eating dead plants, speeding their return to the soil as fertilizer.

Besides, a snail or a slug (which is a snail without a shell) is fun to watch. It has a toothy tongue and one long foot. It is simple to catch and it won't hurt you. If you touch a snail or slug and get some of its slime on your hands, don't worry. Just rub your hands together and the slime will roll into a ball and come off— just like glue.

TRAIL A SNAIL/SLUG

Tools
- Magnifying glass
- Egg flipper

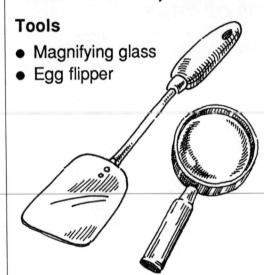

Steps
1. Find a snail or slug on a cool evening. Check damp spots among plants for snails, or look under leaves, rocks or boards for slugs. A silver path of slime left by a snail or slug might lead you to its resting place.

2. GENTLY slide an egg flipper under the animal and place it on the ground. Because you moved it, the snail or slug may pull itself inwards and stay very still.

3. Be patient. Wait until it relaxes and begins to move.

4. Notice the 2 pairs of feelers on its head. Use your magnifying glass to see dark eyes at the tips of the long feelers. These eyes do not see well, but they can tell darkness from light. If the snail or slug senses danger, it may pull its eyes down into its feelers.

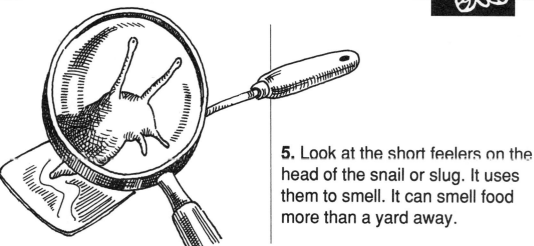

5. Look at the short feelers on the head of the snail or slug. It uses them to smell. It can smell food more than a yard away.

SNAIL AND SLUG SURPRISES

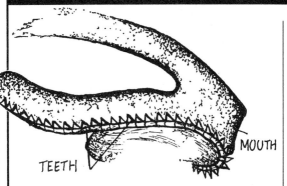

TEETH

MOUTH

- Snails and slugs have hundreds of teeth on their tongues.

- Shortest land snail: $1/16$ inch, just a little wider than a pencil lead.
- Longest land snail: 2 inches, about as long as your little finger.
- A coat of slime protects a snail or slug so well that it can cross broken glass without hurting itself.

LOOK UNDER A SNAIL/SLUG

Tools

- Magnifying glass
- Clear glass dish
- Egg flipper
- A lettuce, spinach or celery leaf

Steps

1. GENTLY slide an egg flipper under a snail or slug, and place the animal into a clear glass dish.

2. Hold up the dish and look at the snail or slug from underneath. Watch how it moves, using the strong muscles in its foot. The muscles ripple from front to back. The snail or slug can travel about 32 inches a minute. As it crawls, it puts out sticky slime to smooth the way.

3. Turn the dish on its edge. Then turn it upside down. The snail or slug hangs on. Its slime helps it move even when it is upside down.

4. Put a lettuce, spinach or celery leaf in front of the snail or slug. Its mouth is underneath, near the small feelers. Use your magnifying glass to watch its tooth-lined tongue scrape off tiny bits from the leaf.

5. Return the snail or slug close to where you found it. It can use its feelers to smell its way back to its resting place. Watch.

NOTHING NICER THAN A TREE

If you have a tree in your backyard, you have more than something beautiful. A living tree gives shade, softens sound and slows wind. It provides food and shelter for many animals. Fruit and nut trees produce food for people. Tree roots help hold the soil. Leaves give off oxygen. Even after parts of a tree die, they help your yard by fertilizing the soil.

There are 2 main kinds of trees: those with broad leaves that drop off in the fall, and those with needles and cones.

This section is about broadleaf trees.

MEET A TREE

Tools
- Notepad and pencil

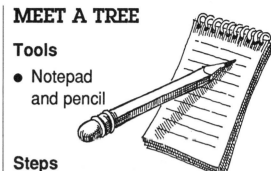

Steps

1. Choose a broadleaf tree in your yard. Run your hand across its "skin"—the tree's bark. It may be thick or thin. It may feel rough or smooth. It may have thin scales or deep ridges. Most young bark is smooth. Older bark may be thicker, with scars and ridges.

2. Check the tree for holes. Try to find some that are big enough for squirrels to use. And look for smaller holes that birds, like woodpeckers, make when they hunt for insects.

3. Sit quietly near the tree and watch it closely for 10 minutes. Use your notepad to keep track of how many different kinds of insects, spiders, birds and other animals you see in the tree.

TREE TRIVIA

- The bigleaf maple produces among the largest leaves in North America. They're up to 1 foot across.
- A big, leafy tree can take in 264 gallons of water in a single day. That's like you drinking all the water from 2 children's backyard swimming pools.

  day. That's like you drinking all the water from 2 children's backyard swimming pools.

4. Compare your notes with the animals you see in the tree on other days.

TAKE A CLOSE LOOK AT A TWIG

Tools

- Magnifying glass

Steps

1. Find a twig on a low-hanging branch of a broadleaf tree. But don't break it off. Look for leaf scars along the twig. Each scar marks a place where a leaf grew before it dropped off in the fall.

LEAF SCAR

BUD

TUBE ENDS

2. Use your magnifying glass to find little dots in each scar. They are the ends of tubes that once brought sap up from the tree's roots. These same tubes took food from the leaf to other parts of the tree.

3. Look for leaf buds on the twig. During winter, they are wrapped in shiny, woolly or hairy covers. In spring, these covers fall off and the buds begin to open. Check to see if the covers are still there.

BUD COVERS

4. Check your twig each day. See how long it takes until the buds are fully open.

5. Now look at how the new leaves are growing. On some trees, leaves grow in clusters. On others, they grow one by one along a twig. Some leaves are divided into lobes; some aren't. Some leaves have smooth edges; some have rough edges.

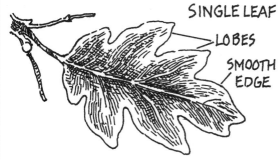

SINGLE LEAF

LOBES

SMOOTH EDGE

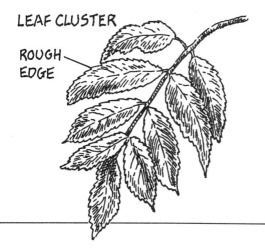

LEAF CLUSTER

ROUGH EDGE

SPARROWS IN SONG

It's easy and fun to find chipping sparrows—also called chippies—in your backyard. In spring and summer, they often stay in gardens and trees close to people. There, they find plenty of food, like seeds, insects, fruit and vegetable matter.

Most people like to have chippies nearby. They add color to the garden. They sing cheerfully. And with training, some may eat out of a person's hand.

SPOT A SPARROW

Steps

1. Watch the birds you see and hear in April and May. Notice their size, color, songs and special features.

2. Pick out a chipping sparrow.
- **Size:** about 5 inches long
- **Color:**
  - streaked brown on the back and grey below
  - bright reddish-brown cap on top of the head
  - black bar out from the eye, white stripe above it
  - white bars on folded wings
- **Tail**: long and slim
- **Bill**: short and cone-shaped
- **Feet:** 3 toes forward and 1 toe back
- **Song:** simple, even set of notes—all sounding the same

3. Watch a chippy find and eat food. The shape of its feet help it perch on a branch or walk across the ground.

4. Listen to a chippy's song. Most songbirds sing only in the morning and evening. But the chipping sparrow often sings all day in early spring.

5. Practise making sounds like a chipping sparrow. When you spot a chippy, stand still and sing its song.

SINGING SUPERSTARS

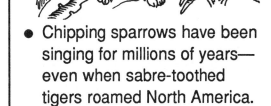

- Chipping sparrows have been singing for millions of years— even when sabre-toothed tigers roamed North America.

- On a spring day, the chipping sparrow is one of the first birds to sing. It often starts 30 minutes before sunrise.
- In early spring, a chippy may sing as many as 330 songs in an hour.

It may answer. Or call to it with a "psssh, psssh, psssh." It may be curious and come closer.

LINE A NEST, WATCH A NEST

Tools

- Strands of hair

Steps

1. Watch for a pair of chipping sparrows building a nest in a bush or shrub, or on a tree branch. They may take 3 or 4 days to build the nest.

2. Gather some strands of hair from brushes and combs in your house. Check pet brushes, too.

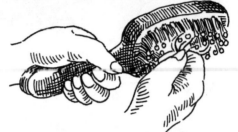

3. Leave the strands of hair on the ground near the nest or on a clothesline. Chippies make nests from bits of rootlets, twigs and grasses, but they like to line their nests with hair.

4. Check to see if the chippies take the strands. But don't go too close to the nest. In May, June or July, chipping sparrows will lay 3 to 5 small, spotted, bluish eggs in the nest. The eggs hatch in about 10 days.

5. Try to see what chippies feed their young. They may offer more insects than seeds.

RAIN, RAIN, COME AGAIN

It's a good thing there is always water in the air. That means rain is always forming. Plants, animals and people need rain—even if it does spoil a picnic.

The air over some parts of Earth is much damper than it is over other parts. But wherever tiny droplets of water in the air bump into each other, they join together. Gradually, they grow bigger and heavier until they fall as rain.

FLIP-FLOP IN A DROP

Steps

1. Look closely at a raindrop on a leaf or petal. Notice the shape of the drop.

2. Find something reflected in the drop: a tree, a bush or you. What you see is upside down—unlike what you see in a mirror. It's the shape of the raindrop that makes the difference.

PREDICT THE RAIN

Tools

- Radio
- Notepad and pencil

Steps

1. Listen to the radio weather report in the morning.

2. If the reporter expects rain that day, look in your yard for signs that rain is coming.

- Many flowers close before rain. Check dandelions and tulips.

- Some trees turn their leaves over.
- Clover plants pull their leaves together.
- Some spiders take down their webs before really heavy rain.

3. Listen for clear noises. Sound travels better in damp air.

4. Smell the air. Some people say they can smell things better in damp air. Watch a dog to see if it's smelling the air.

5. List all the things that happen in your yard before it rains. Check the list on many days. Erase things that don't always happen before it rains. Add other things that do.

6. Try to predict rain **BEFORE** you turn on the radio in the morning.

RAIN REVIEW

- A raindrop is shaped more like a bun than a teardrop.

- Giant raindrops, $5/16$ inch across, have fallen in Hawaii. They are about as wide as your little fingernail. Most raindrops are only about $1/16$ inch across.

- Mt. Waialeale on the island of Kauai, Hawaii, gets the most rain in the United States—about 460 inches a year. That would fill a building 4 stories tall.

DANDELIONS ARE DANDY

Check your yard for a lion's tooth—a dandelion, really. Its name comes from *dent de lion*, which is French for "tooth of a lion." The dandelion was named for its leaves that look like sharp teeth. It is one of the first wildflowers you see in the spring.

To most gardeners, the dandelion is only a weed. But some people use parts of it for salads, teas and other drinks, and many animals feed on it. Birds, for example, eat dandelion seeds, and insects drink the nectar.

DIVIDE A DANDELION

Tools

- Magnifying glass

Steps

1. Look at a dandelion's jagged leaves. They don't grow from the stem like leaves on many plants do. They grow from the roots and spread across the ground. That keeps other plants from crowding around the dandelion.

2. Pick a dandelion flower. Break it in half—lengthwise—and look closely with your magnifying glass. The flower is really a lot of tiny flowers growing side by side, the smallest ones in the middle.

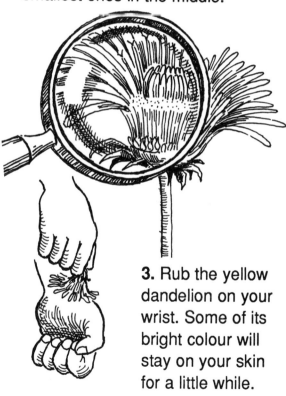

3. Rub the yellow dandelion on your wrist. Some of its bright colour will stay on your skin for a little while.

4. Break off the stem and look inside. It's as hollow as a straw, so strong winds can't snap it.

5. Split the stem open and feel the sticky, white juice. Cows and sheep find this juice bitter, so they don't eat dandelions.

FOLLOW THAT SEED

Tools

- Magnifying glass

Steps

1. Find dandelion flowers that have

DANDELION DATA

- Early explorers from Europe brought the first dandelions to North America.
- One full dandelion bloom can produce 180 seeds.
- Any small bit of dandelion root, left in the ground, can produce a new plant.

closed up and dried. Break one open. You can see tiny, green seeds growing beneath the little flowers.

2. Look for dandelion flowers that have opened again after their petals have died. They look like fluffy white balls. Carefully break one open and look at the seeds. They have turned brown.

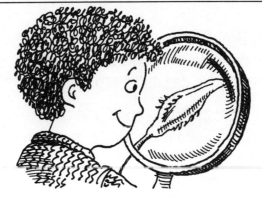

3. Feel a single seed. It is light, hard and sharp. Use your magnifying glass to spot its tiny hooks. They help the seed take hold of a place to grow.

4. Notice a white, hair-like parachute attached to each seed. When the wind blows, these parachutes glide through the air, taking seeds to new spots.

5. GENTLY pick a fluffy dandelion and blow its parachutes. Follow one or two to see where they land. If one lands in soil—even in a crack in a sidewalk or driveway—it may grow a new dandelion plant.

WHAT BIRDS DO

Finding out what birds do is more fun than just learning their names. You can learn about bird behavior the same way scientists do—by watching and listening.

Some of the most exciting behavior involves all the things that birds do with—or to—each other. For instance, a robin may sing "tut-tut-tut" to warn other robins of danger. It might even share its nest with other kinds of birds. A pair of robins and a pair of mourning doves have been seen together— building a single nest, laying their eggs and caring for their young.

WAIT, WATCH AND LISTEN

Steps

1. Wear clothes that are dull or light in color. Go outside in early morning or late afternoon when birds are busiest.

2. Choose a spot where you won't disturb the birds. Sit where you are partly hidden, but where you can see clearly.

3. Be patient. Birds have quiet times between busy times.

4. Watch and listen closely. Note how one bird reacts or calls to another.

BRING ON THE BIRDS

Tools

- Plastic ice cream pail with lid
- Small nail
- Strong cardboard box

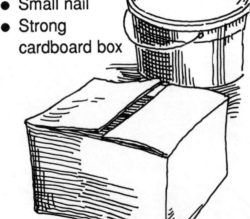

Steps

1. Create a slow-drip tub and drinking hole for birds. Use a nail to punch a small hole in the bottom of the pail—about an inch from the edge.

2. Set the box where the birds like to gather. Put the lid—upside down—beside the box. Stand the pail mostly on the box so that the hole is above the lid. Fill the pail half-full of water and let it drip slowly into the lid.

3. Sit away from the pail and watch birds enjoy the shallow, moving water.

4. Try to attract other birds to your yard by making noises that make them curious.
- Open and close your lips while saying "shhh."
- Suck air through your lips.
- Noisily kiss your hand.

BIRDS CALLING

- Many birds can sing up to 15 different songs. Some can sing as many as 25. Most songs mean something like, "Keep out. This is my area."
- Birds also use songs to report food, attract mates, scare enemies or warn each other of danger.

SUNSHINE IS GOLD

The sun is a huge globe of burning gasses about 93 million miles away. Even though it's so far, the sun gives our planet heat and light. That makes it possible for plants to grow, and for animals and people to live on Earth.

Heat and light from the sun affect people in many little ways, too. For example, light affects what people see, and heat affects how they work and play. Too much sunshine can even make people sick.

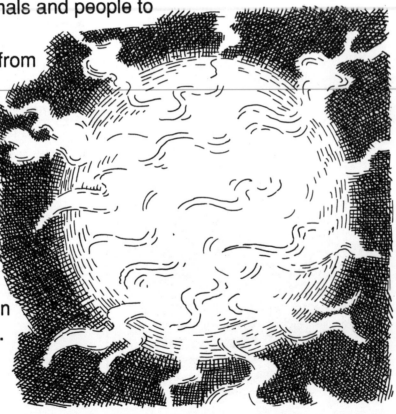

SEE SUNSHINE AFFECT YOU

Tools

- Hand mirror

Steps

1. See sunshine change your eyes.
- Sit in a darkened room and look closely in a mirror at your pupils (the black centers of your eyes).

- Step out into bright sunshine. Look around, but do **NOT** look directly at the sun. After a few minutes, check your pupils in a hand mirror. They will be much smaller now. In bright light, pupils become smaller to reduce the amount of light entering the eyes.

2. See sunshine affect the colors you see.
- Look at the colors of things in shady parts of your yard.
- Look at the colors of things in sunny areas. They look

SUN FUN

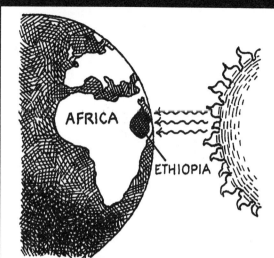

- Hottest place on Earth: Dallol, Ethiopia, where the average temperature during the year is about 94° Fahrenheit.

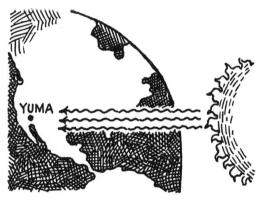

- Sunniest place in the U.S.: Yuma, Arizona, with about 4,000 hours of sunshine a year.

- Age of the sun: about 5 billion years.

brighter. Light makes it possible for you to see colors.
- Look out the window at your yard at night. Notice how little color you see.

3. See sunshine change your shadow.
- Check it at 9:00 A.M. It's long and points westward.

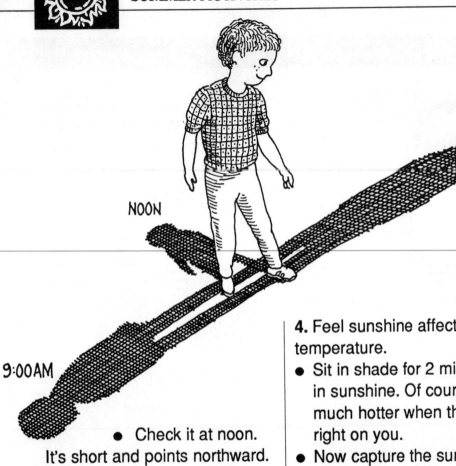

4:00PM

NOON

9:00AM

- Check it at noon.
  It's short and points northward.
- Check it at 4:00 P.M. It's long and points eastward.
  The angle of the sunshine changes your shadow.

4. Feel sunshine affect your temperature.
- Sit in shade for 2 minutes, then in sunshine. Of course, you feel much hotter when the sun shines right on you.
- Now capture the sunshine in your clothes: wear something black and sit in the sunshine. Black absorbs light and heat, and that makes you warmer.

- Change into something white. It reflects light and heat, and that keeps you cooler.

5. Feel sunshine steal your energy.
- Try to notice and remember how you feel when the temperature is cool (around 65° Fahrenheit) and when it is very hot (at least 95° Fahrenheit). Compare. Strong heat usually makes people feel sluggish.

WORM WAYS

Wriggly earthworms live in countries all over the world. Some live in your backyard. You see them on lawns or roads on rainy days. But usually, worms live underground in cool, damp soil where they stay moist. Worms breathe through their skins. If they dry out, the worms die.

Earthworms have no eyes, no ears, no nose, no teeth, no legs and no bones. But they are some of the world's most important animals. They plough the soil, letting in air and water. As they tunnel along, they swallow soil and dead plant and animal matter. Then they create little piles of soil mixed with waste. All this helps plants grow, making food for animals and people.

UNEARTH AN EARTHWORM

Tools
- Small shovel or trowel
- Newspaper

Steps

1. Go outside on a dark, cloudy day. Earthworms avoid light.

2. Walk softly. Worms sense your footsteps.

3. Dig in a damp place in a garden, or beneath a tree or rock.

4. Dump big scoops of soil on a newspaper.

5. Spread out the soil. **GENTLY** feel for a large worm.

6. Hold the worm and put the soil back.

BE A WORM WHIZ

Tools
- Magnifying glass

Steps

1. Feel how soft and moist the earthworm is.

2. Look at the 100 to 200 muscle rings in its body.

3. Find the worm's head and tail by looking for a wide, light-colored band. It is closer to the head.

4. Find the worm's top and bottom. No matter how you place the worm, it will turn itself topside up.

5. Gently slide your finger along the bottom of the worm—from tail to head. You can feel hundreds of tiny bristles. They help the worm move.

They also help it hold tight to its underground burrow if a bird tries to pull the worm out.

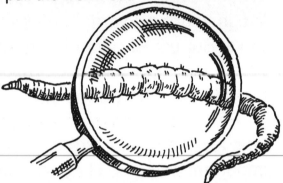

6. Use your magnifying glass to see the bristles.

WATCH A WORM

Tools
- Cake pan
- 4 sheets of toilet paper, stacked and dampened

Steps

1. Put the damp toilet paper over part of the pan.

2. GENTLY place the earthworm—half on the pan, half on the paper. Watch which way it moves.

3. Do this several times. The worm will prefer the paper. It is damp and uneven—like soil. The pan is smooth and hard to grip with bristles.

4. Watch how the worm moves. It stretches its front end out like an elastic, then the tail end follows.

5. Release the worm where you found it and watch it burrow back into the soil, or under leaves or rocks.

6. Lie face down on the grass, your legs together, arms by your sides. Try to move like a worm.

WONDER WORMS AROUND THE WORLD

- Worms can move 50 times their weight. That's like you pushing a rhinoceros.
- 50,000 worms can live in a big backyard.
- There are about 3,000 kinds of earthworms.
- Longest earthworm: about $11\frac{1}{2}$ feet, almost as long as 2 beds placed end to end.
- Shortest earthworm: about $\frac{1}{32}$ inch, the width of a pencil lead.

THE AIR WE BREATHE

Plants, animals and people need air to live. But when it contains lots of pollutants, air can be harmful. Pollutants in air are gases and bits of things, like ash, soot, dust, pollen, salt, weeds, rock and smoke. They can clog tiny leaf openings that plants breathe through. And they can make it hard for people and animals to breathe.

Air pollution is usually worse in the city. Many cities have 5 to 10 times more pollutants than country areas have. Most of these pollutants come from traffic, homes, garbage dumps, factories and mills. Sometimes, air pollutants are so thick they decrease the amount of sunlight that reaches cities.

TRAP POLLUTANTS

Tools

- Wax paper
- Scissors
- 8 thumb tacks
- Petroleum jelly (sold under various brand names, like Vaseline)
- Magnifying glass

Steps

1. Cut out 2 squares of wax paper—each about 6 inches long and 6 inches wide.

AIR CARES

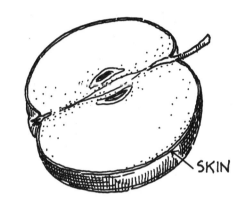

SKIN

AIR

- The layer of air around Earth is as thin as skin is to an apple. The air we breathe is used over and over again.
- Scientists in China found signs of air pollution in the lungs of a 3,000-year-old mummy.
- Cars, trucks and busses cause most of the air pollution in cities.
- In one year, trees in an area the size of an average city block can remove 14.3 tons of dust and gasses from the air. That's about as much as some large, fully loaded gravel trucks weigh.

2. Tack the squares to a fence, pole or post—some place out in the open. Put one square in the front yard and one in the back or side yard.

3. Smear both squares evenly with petroleum jelly.

4. After a week, look for material stuck to the squares. Use your magnifying glass. Check for signs of natural pollution (bits of weed, rock and dust) and human pollution (ash, soot and bits of paper). Of course, you can't see pollutants that are gases. The squares might also pick up small insects.

5. Compare the 2 squares. The one closer to traffic may have picked up more—or different—pollutants than the other. If neither square has picked up much, you are lucky to be living where you are.

6. Try this experiment again in the fall when houses are being heated and leaves are being burned. You may find more pollutants.

LADYBUG LUCK

Ladybugs are lucky bugs. Lucky for us, that is. They eat plant-sucking aphids and other insects that attack food crops, bushes and trees. And they are BIG eaters. Even when ladybugs are young, they eat so much they are called aphid-wolves.

Years ago, people believed ladybugs were lucky in other ways: bringing good weather, making marriages, curing sickness and ending toothaches. But ladybugs are beetles, not magicians. They simply help us by doing what ladybugs do best. They eat.

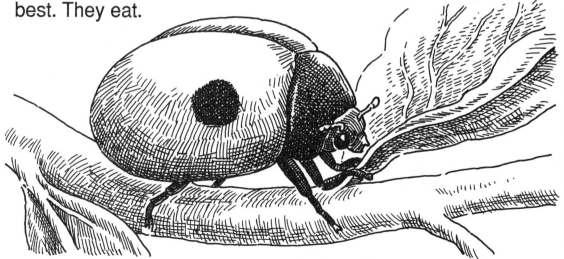

LOOK A LADYBUG OVER

Tools

- Magnifying glass

Steps

1. Look for a ladybug on a tree, bush (especially a rosebush) or a vegetable, like peas or corn. Note the ladybug's body: oval with thick, shiny, spotted wing covers. Count the spots, which formed less than 12 hours after the ladybug became an adult. The number of spots tells you which kind of ladybug it is—not its age, as people often think. Its bright colour warns others that ladybugs are not good-tasting.

LOWDOWN ON LADYBUGS

- In cold weather, ladybugs often gather beneath moss, leaves or rocks. Up to 750 million ladybugs may be found in one spot.
- There are about 4000 different kinds of ladybugs. They may be red, brown, yellow or white.
- Just 12 ladybugs can eat enough insect pests to save a fruit tree.

2. Get a cat to sniff the ladybug, and watch how the cat reacts. It will likely find the smell disgusting.

3. Use your magnifying glass to study the ladybug's small head: large eyes, short feelers with knobs on the ends and a mouth. And check its legs. Like all insects, it has 6. Each is short and built for running.

4. Watch how a ladybug moves on a plant. It tends to crawl on the edges of leaves, or along the raised lines.

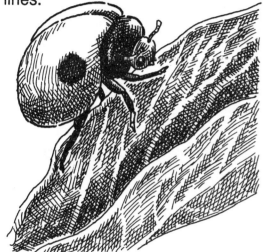

5. See if the ladybug catches something to eat. After it eats, it may clean its face with its front legs. Then it cleans those legs with its jaws.

PLAY WITH A LADYBUG

Steps

1. Let the ladybug walk up your finger onto your hand. Feel its tiny feet tickle your skin.

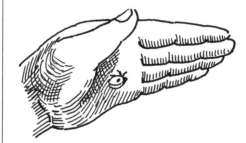

2. Turn your hand over slowly and watch the ladybug walk upside down. Sticky pads on its feet make that possible.

3. On a flat part of your hand, **GENTLY** roll the ladybug onto its back. When a ladybug feels threatened by a spider or ant, it may lie on its back and play dead.

4. Watch the ladybug use its spotted wing covers to turn right side up. Once it is upright, you may see the tips of the wings hanging below the covers. The ladybug will soon tuck them in again.

WING
TIP ———

5. Blow lightly to make the ladybug fly away. Watch it hold up the wing covers and fly using its big, clear wings. It looks very awkward, but the ladybug flies just fine this way.

FLOWERS: THE SEED FACTORIES

Flowers provide food for many insects, birds and bigger animals, like deer. They also add beauty to our homes, gardens and parks. But flowers are even more important to the plants that produce them, because flowers are seed factories. Without them, many kinds of plants would never grow again.

Most flowers need pollen from other flowers to produce seeds. Wind moves pollen by blowing it, and insects carry pollen from blossom to blossom. This is called "fertilizing."

DOGWOOD

FIGURE A FLOWER

Steps

1. Look at the petals in a large flower. The bright colors attract insects to the flower's sweet nectar. The smell of some flowers also attracts insects. But the pollen of some—like many grass flowers—is spread by wind, and these flowers often have no petals at all.

2. Find the pistil—the tube in the center. There may be more than one. The pistil is the female part that produces seeds.

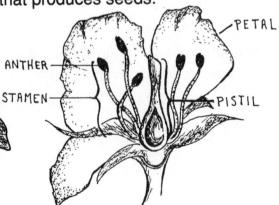

PETAL

ANTHER

STAMEN

PISTIL

3. Check the stamens—long thin rods with fuzzy tops, called anthers. These are the male parts that produce pollen—the yellow powder. Insects are brushed with pollen when they pick up nectar.

POLLINATE A FLOWER

Tools

● 2 pencils

Steps

1. Choose a flower with stamens and pistils that you can see easily.

2. GENTLY touch the tip of the stamen with a pencil, picking up some pollen.

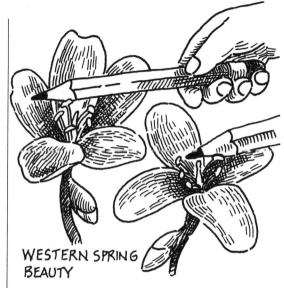

WESTERN SPRING BEAUTY

3. Move the pencil to another flower of the same kind, and touch the tip of its pistil. Some of the pollen will rub off onto the pistil.

4. Try to remove some pollen by touching the same pistil with another pencil. It won't pick up much because the pistil is sticky or feathery. That helps the flower keep the pollen it needs to produce seeds.

FLOWER POWER

● A single lily blossom in Malaysia weighs up to 13 pounds—as much as a fox.

● Some grass flowers are so small you need a microscope to see one.

● One flower may produce thousands—even millions—of grains of pollen.

● Some flowers smell stronger at night so moths can find them.

THOSE INCREDIBLE INSECTS

Insects have lived on Earth for hundreds of millions of years. They live in and on soil, water, plants, animals—even snow and ice. They live on every continent.

Few insects cause people harm, and many are useful. They pollinate flowers, provide food for many animals and help keep the soil healthy. Some control harmful insects. Others provide special things, like silk from silk worms (which grow into moths) and honey from bees.

HUNT FOR INSECTS

Tools

- Magnifying glass
- Small shovel or trowel
- Umbrella

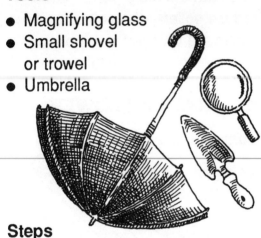

Steps

1. See how many kinds of insects you can find in your backyard (one scientist found more than 1000 in his yard).

- Look under rocks and fallen leaves.
- Dig in the soil.
- Look in the air.
- Check in the grass, and on flowers, plants and trees.

• Choose a little shrub and—in 5 minutes—see how many kinds of insects you can find. Use your magnifying glass to spot small ones.

2. Listen for insects that make noise. Houseflies buzz by beating their wings up to 20 000 times a minute. Grasshoppers click by rubbing their legs and wings together. Crickets chirp by drawing one wing across the other.

3. Hold an open umbrella upside down and hook a low tree branch with the handle. Shake the branch a few times or hit it hard with a stick. Insects will tumble into the umbrella.

INSECT INSIGHTS

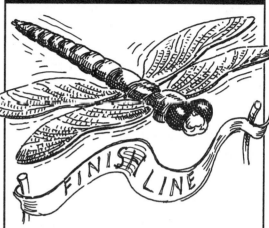

• The dragonfly is one of the fastest flying insects on Earth.

• A flea can jump up to 130 times its height. That's like you jumping as high as a 60-story building.

• There are twice as many kinds of insects as there are all other kinds of animals put together.

INSPECT INSECTS

Tools

- Magnifying glass

Steps

1. Compare the insects you find. Adults each have 6 legs and 3 body sections. On their heads, many have feelers, used for smelling and—on some insects—for tasting or hearing. Large feelers may pick up smells that are far away.

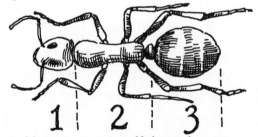

2. Use your magnifying glass to see other parts. Many insects have mouthparts for chewing or sucking. For example, a grasshopper uses

BREATHING PORE

jaws to chew grass, and a mosquito sticks a tube into skin to suck blood. Most insects have many eyes (some beetles have 25 000). But don't look for a nose. An insect breathes through small pores along its body. You may be able to see them on a large insect, like a grasshopper.

RACE A WINNER

Tools

- Chalk or a soft rock
- Garbage can lid

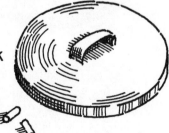

Steps

1. Make an insect racetrack. Place the garbage can lid on a driveway or sidewalk. Trace around the lid. Now draw a large dot in the middle of this circle.

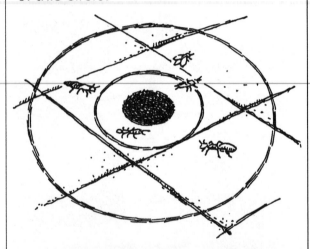

2. Place about 5 insects in the inner circle near the dot. Watch to see which one reaches the big circle first. Try another race. Then put the insects back where you found them.

ECOSYSTEM DETECTIVE

Scientists often learn about nature by studying an ecosystem—all the living and non-living things in a particular place. That place may be big like a forest, or small like a log. Whatever its size, scientists look at how the things in an ecosystem affect each other. When you explore nature in your backyard, you are learning about ecosystems, too. So grab your magnifying glass and be an ecosystem detective.

EXPLORE A MINI-WORLD

Tools

- Plastic ice cream pail lid
- Magnifying glass
- Notepad and pencil

Steps

1. Find a little section of a grassy ecosystem to study by tossing a lid across the lawn. Where it lands, press down on it. The pressure will make a light circle.

2. Look very closely within the circle. Check under stones, between blades of grass, and so on. Use your magnifying glass. List all the things you see: stones, soil, plants, animals, bits of dead plants and animals, things that animals have left—like eggs or webs.

Is it gritty or smooth, dry or damp? Stick your pencil in the soil to see how hard or soft it is.

4. Toss the plastic lid to a different part of your lawn and study another little circle within the grassy

3. Write down anything you notice. Count the kinds of each thing you see. Note which insects eat the plants—or each other. Feel the soil.

EXCITING ECOSYSTEMS

- Hundreds of animals can live in an ecosystem beneath a rock.

- Tiny, tiny insects and other animals in underground ecosystems change Earth's huge ecosystem by adding wastes to the soil and removing minerals.
- City ecosystems replace natural ecosystems, even changing climates. Most cities have warmer nights, cloudier days, slower wind, and more rain than the nearby countryside.

ecosystem. Compare it with the first. Think of reasons for the differences. For instance, one might be sunnier or wetter than the other.

MAKE A WILD PLACE

Tools

- 4 wooden sticks or chopsticks
- String
- Notepad and pencil

Steps

1. Ask for permission to let a small corner of your lawn stay untouched for a few weeks.

2. Measure an area about 12 inches by 12 inches, poking sticks into the ground at each corner. Tie string around the sticks—as shown below.

3. Make a list of all the plants, animals or signs of animals you find within the grassy square.

4. Do not pull weeds, rake leaves or step inside the square.

5. Check it once a week and make more lists of what you find. Note changes. Because your grassy wild place is not disturbed, more animals and plants may move in.

THE ANTS GO MARCHING

There are thousands of different kinds of ants on Earth. But all kinds are social, which means they live and work together. That's what makes ants unlike most other insects. And that's why so many scientists want to learn more about ants.

All the ants that live in one nest come from the eggs of one ant—the queen. She looks after her first set of ants until they grow. Then they look after her and the other eggs she lays. Soon there are more and more of these worker ants. They find food for the ant colony, protect the young, clean the nest and so on.

ANALYZE AN ANT

Tools

- Magnifying glass

Steps

1. Watch for an ant on a warm fall day. Ants usually don't leave their nests if it's colder than 54° Fahrenheit.

2. Follow that ant and see what it does. When it stops, use your magnifying glass to see its big eyes and the feelers it uses to smell and touch. You may see it clean its feelers, pulling them through long leg hairs. Ants clean themselves often.

3. Check the ant's mouth—designed to chew, dig, build, carry and fight. And try to see its claws, which help the ant climb trees.

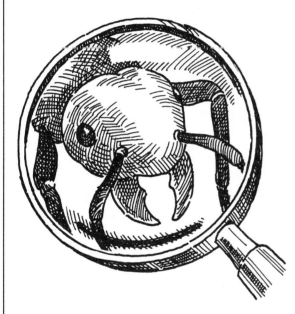

4. Make a small puddle of water in front of an ant, blocking its way. Notice how it avoids water and walks around the puddle. Ants can drown in water.

5. Find an ant nest. Look under a rock or some firewood. If you uncover a nest, you may see many worker ants running for safety. **GENTLY** set the rock or firewood back the way it was. The ants will return when they sense it's safe.

ANT ANTICS

- An ant can lift 50 times its own weight. That's like you lifting a rhinoceros.
- Some farming ants grow their own food—a fungus. They chew up leaves to make fertilizer for their gardens.
- Shortest worker ant: about 0.3 inches, less than the width of a pencil lead.
- Longest worker ant: about $1\frac{1}{4}$ inches, slightly longer than the average paper clip.

TREAT AN ANT

Tools

- Honey
- Bread crust
- A juicy fruit, like a pear

Steps

1. Dip a small bit of bread crust in honey and drop it in front of an ant.

2. Watch closely to see if the ant carries the food in its mouth or eats it. If the ant eats the food, it may go into the ant's second stomach, which is used to carry food back to the nest.

3. Place half of a juicy fruit near some ants. They may suck out some of the juice with their mouths, then go back to the nest. Because they're excited about finding the fruit, their bodies leave a trail along the way. You can't see it, but the ants in the nest can smell it. They will likely follow the trail to the fruit.

4. Watch to see if more and more ants come to the fruit. Count the number that come. See how long it takes them to suck most of the fruit.

MORE THAN DIRT

Soil is not just dirt. It contains rock material, bits of rotting plants and animals, air and water. The amount of each depends on the place and the year—even within your backyard.

Much life depends on soil. Plants need it to grow, and people and animals need plants for food. Yet the soil that covers Earth is usually no more than four feet thick.

SORT THE SOLID STUFF

Tools

- Small shovel or trowel
- Newspaper

Steps

1. Dig a hole about a foot deep in soil under a tree or bush. Place the soil on newspapers and spread it out.

2. Discover what your soil is made of. Sort it into 3 piles of rock, plant and animal matter.

- Rock matter is made up of stones, sand and fine dirt called silt and clay.
- Plant matter is made up of roots, twigs, leaves, berries and seeds.
- Animal matter can be feathers, bits of insects or tiny bones.

3. On one side of the hole, use your shovel to make a smooth wall. Look for layers in the wall. Dark layers at the top, called topsoil, contain the most plant and animal matter,

NATURAL LITTER   TOPSOIL

SUBSOIL

which helps plants grow. Lower layers, called subsoil, are lighter colors and contain bigger bits of rock. Larger roots reach into these lower layers to hold plants in place. Beneath the soil lies a layer of rock called bedrock. A 1-foot hole will not likely reach bedrock.

4. Put all the soil back into the hole.

FIND SIGNS OF WATER AND AIR

Tools

- Glass jar
- Wooden spoon
- Magnifying glass

Steps

1. Scoop some soil into a jar until it's nearly full.

2. Slowly add water, letting it soak into the soil. Watch bubbles form at the top of the water. Many bubbles or big bubbles mean that the soil had lots of air in it. When the water filled in the tiny spaces between the grains of soil, it pushed the air out.

3. Take handfuls of soil from different parts of your yard. Squeeze each handful into a ball

STORIES OF SAND AND SOIL

- It takes hundreds of years for an inch of new topsoil to form naturally.

- Tiny grains of sand change very little—even thousands of years after breaking off from their parent rock.
- Some kinds of stones, called lodestones, are like magnets. Iron nails will cling to these stones.

and compare them. The balls that stick together have more water in them. They may contain lots of silt or clay, which absorbs water. Soil that holds little water crumbles. It may contain lots of sand, which absorbs water very poorly. With your magnifying glass, you may be able to see bits of sand.

DRIER SOIL

MOISTER SOIL

4. Remember to put all the soil back.

CHEERS FOR CHICKADEES

A buzz sounds like "buz-z-z." A splash sounds like "splash-sh." And a chickadee sounds like "chick-a-dee." That's how the bird got its name—from the song it sings.

Chickadees often visit backyards, so watch for them at your place. They're nice birds to have around—full of energy and song. They look cute, too, with their black caps and bibs. And as they flit among trees and bushes, chickadees eat some of the insects that attack gardens.

CHECK UP ON CHICKADEES

Tools
- Sunflower seeds

Steps

1. Look and listen for chickadees in your yard. The most common kind is the black-capped chickadee. It is described below. Other kinds of chickadees are slightly different.
- **Size:** about 4½ to 5 inches long
- **Color:** • gray back
    - black cap and bib
    - white patch on face
- **Tail:** slender
- **Bill:** stubby and small
- **Feet:** 3 toes forward and 1 toe back
- **Song:** a whistle

2. Watch chickadees hunting and eating insects in bushes and trees. The most powerful ones feed first.

3. Try feeding a chickadee from your hand.

- Put a few sunflower seeds on your palm.

- Extend your hand to a chickadee. Be very quiet and patient—super patient.
- Try each day until a chickadee takes a seed.

CHICKADEE DEEDS

- Chickadees hang around—upside down on branches. They can even feed that way.
- A flock of chickadees will chase other flocks out of its area.
- When a flock of chickadees must cross an open space, just one bird crosses at a time.

4. Watch the chickadee take the seed to a branch to eat. See how the bird holds the seed while pecking at it.

IT'S A BREEZE!

Wind is more than moving air. Wind is energy. For people, it moves sailboats, turns windmills and dries laundry. In nature, it spreads seeds, shifts soil and dries puddles.

When warm air rises, cold air moves in under it, causing wind. If the difference between warm and cold air is great, the wind blows hard and fast. In 1805, a British admiral, Sir Francis Beaufort, made a simple chart to help people rate the speed of wind.

Beaufort Wind Chart with speeds in miles per hour (mph)

0   Smoke rises
    straight up
    0 mph

1   Smoke drifts
    to one side
    1-3 mph

2   Leaves rustle
    Flag waves gently
    4-7 mph

3   Twigs & leaves
    moves
    8-12 mph

4   Small branches
    move
    Dust rises
    13-18 mph

5   Small trees sway
    Clothes snap on the line
    19-24 mph

6   Large branches
    move
    25-31 mph

7   Whole trees
    move
    32-38 mph

8   Twigs break
    Walking is hard
    39-46 mph

9   Slight damage
    to trees
    47-54 mph

10 Trees uproot
    Much damage
    55-63 mph

11 Heavy damage
    to buildings
    64-75 mph

12 Widespread
    destruction
    76 mph and up

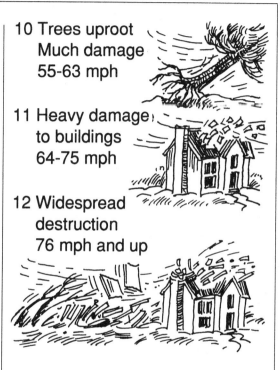

TRACK THE WIND

Tools

- Calendar
- Pencil

Steps

1. Sense the wind. You can't see it, but your eyes, ears, and body let you know where it is and what it's like. Hear it howl along rooftops or who-o-osh among leaves. Watch how plants and animals act in the wind. Feel its strength on your back and its temperature on your face.

2. Visit your yard the same time each day for a week or two, and compare the wind with the Beaufort Wind Chart. Choose the number of the description that best fits the wind. Write it on the calendar. Note how the wind changes through the week(s).

3. Hold a big leaf above your head, then drop it. Watch where it goes: it might go straight down, part-way or all the way across the yard or outside the yard. Write that down beside the Beaufort number on the calendar. Notice how the wind's strength changes the leaf's movement.

WILD IS THE WIND

- Hot, dry chinook winds—common just east of the Rocky Mountains—can increase winter temperatures 40° Fahrenheit in a few hours.
- Windiest spot on Earth: Commonwealth Bay, Antarctica.

ALONG CAME A SPIDER

There are thousands of different kinds of spiders—different shapes, sizes, colors, and designs. They eat different foods, which they catch different ways—some at night, some during the day.

People often feel afraid of spiders—of the way they look or the sudden way they move. But very few kinds of spiders can hurt people. In fact, spiders are really helpful. They are one of nature's best pest controls because they eat so many insects.

SPY A SPIDER

Tools

● Magnifying glass

Steps

1. Find a medium-to-large spider in your yard. Check in shrubs and along tree trunks. Or look on or near a web to see if the spider that made it is there. Common garden spiders often build webs near houses, in open, sunny spots.

2. Do not pick up the spider, but take a close look at it. Note the colors and designs on its body. And check to see if the spider is generally smooth or hairy.

3. Notice that it is not an insect. Spiders have only 2 body sections and 8 legs; insects have 3 body sections and 6 legs.

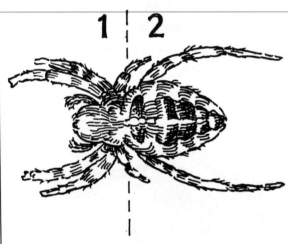

4. Use your magnifying glass to see the spider's head. Look for the eyes. Many spiders have 8 eyes,

but even so, they may not see well. Check for the pointed fangs used to grab insects. Near the tip of each fang, there is a tiny opening where liquid comes out. Spiders use this liquid to paralyze insects.

WATCH A WEB

Steps

1. Find a big, round web—untorn and empty of insects. Notice the design. It may be simple or complex. But most spiders can spin a web in less than an hour. Many spin one each night.

2. GENTLY touch an outside thread or the thread that connects the web to the tree, fence or other support. Notice the thread is not sticky.

3. Now **GENTLY** touch a thread on the main part of the web. It sticks to your finger. Most spiders make more than one kind of silk. Besides building webs, they use silk for things like wrapping eggs and the insects that are caught in the webs.

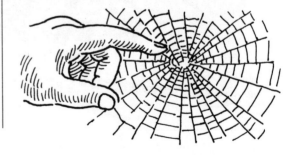

4. Notice that the spider will probably come out from its nearby hiding place when you touch the web. A spider stays attached to its web by a thin, silk thread. That way, it can sense the smallest movement.

5. After the spider returns to its hiding place, toss a bit of grass into the sticky center of the web. The spider will likely run to it, then discover that the grass is not food. The spider will remove it, then wait for an insect.

WONDER WEBS, SPECIAL SPIDERS

- The webs that spiders spin can be as tiny as a postage stamp or as large as a man.
- The silk in webs is one of Earth's strongest materials. If you made it into rope, it would be stronger than steel cable.
- Earth's smallest spider is half the size of the period at the end of this sentence.
- The legs of Earth's biggest spider would hang over a large dinner plate.

6. Watch to see if an insect gets caught in the web. If it does, the spider will rush in and bite it, then wrap the insect in silk. Later, the spider will suck the juices from the insect, leaving the skin behind.

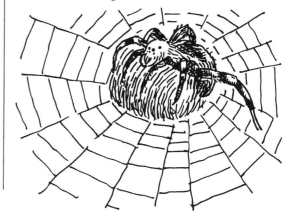

SEEDS ON THE MOVE

Seeds take interesting trips. They move from their parent plant to spots where they can grow. That way, new plants get started. Of course, seeds can't move themselves, but they get around in many ways.

- Most seeds travel by air. The wind blows very small ones. Some seeds have "wings" that help them glide.

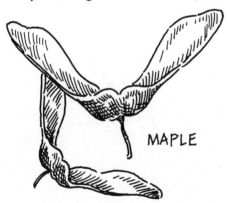

MAPLE

BURDOCK

- Sticky or prickly seeds cling to animals' fur or people's clothes. The seeds get scratched off or picked off later.

- Birds scatter some of the seeds they find for food.

MOUNTAIN ASH

SEEK OUT SOME SEEDS

Tools
- Magnifying glass

Steps

1. Look for seeds in your yard. Check trees, bushes, weeds and flowers.

2. Compare them to the seeds in this section. Figure out how each of them might move.

3. Toss seeds with "wings." Watch how far they travel.

4. Feel prickly seeds that would stick to your socks. Use your magnifying glass to see what makes them stick.

5. Watch birds eat seeds—or berries with seeds. After they leave, check for seeds or berries that the birds have dropped. You may need to use your magnifying glass.

SUPER SEED SEND-OFFS

- Tumbleweed seeds travel with their parent plant. Wind uproots the whole tumbleweed and rolls it along the ground.

- Wind can blow tiny seeds hundreds of miles.
- Grass seeds can rise more than 3,000 feet into the air.
- A miner in Canada's Yukon found some frozen seeds. He took them to a scientist who was able to grow them—even though they were 10000 years old!

LET IT SNOW!

Snow falls on every continent on Earth. Generally, in warm places, it only falls on very tall mountains. In northern states, it falls almost everywhere every winter.

Snow is pretty, and it's fun to play in. But to many plants and animals, snow is survival. Like a blanket, it protects them from freezing temperatures and harsh winds. And when snow melts, it releases water to soil and streams.

KNOW THE SNOW

Tools

- Magnifying glass

Steps

1. Go outside when it is snowing. Use your magnifying glass to study the snowflakes that land on your sleeve.

2. Compare their patterns. Each one is unique, and each one changes in less than a minute. Notice that snowflakes get rounder as they melt.

MELT THE SNOW

Tools

- 2 clear plastic containers of the same size
- Ruler
- Salt

Steps

1. Completely fill one plastic container with snow. Measure the depth of the snow with your ruler.

2. Stand the snow in your garage or house until it all melts. Measure the depth of the remaining water.

3. Compare the depth of snow with the depth of water. There may be about 10 times more snow. Snow is mostly air.

4. Half-fill 2 plastic containers with snow. Add about a handful of salt to one container.

5. Keep checking to see which melts first. Salt helps melt snow. That is why people sometimes put salt on snowy sidewalks and roads.

WINTER WONDERLAND

- Just 10 inches of snow covering 1 or 2 of the yards on your street can weigh 44,000 pounds—about as much as 4 elephants.
- Some snowflakes are 10 inches across—almost as wide as this page.
- Tiny plants, called algae, can grow in snow. They make the snow look red or pink.

DIG A DRIFT

Tools

- Shovel
- Outdoor thermometer

Steps

1. Look for snowdrifts in your yard. The wind makes drifts by blowing snow against and behind trees, poles, fences and sheds. Choose one drift to study.

2. With a shovel, **GENTLY** slice straight through the drift—right to the ground. Then look for layers where wind and snow have built up the drift. Each layer may be a slightly different colour.

3. Feel the snow in the layers and compare. For example, some layers may feel smooth, others gritty.

4. Notice the temperature of the winter air on a thermometer. Then take the temperature of the snow halfway down the drift and, again, at the bottom of the drift. Compare these 3 temperatures. The warmest temperature will be at the ground. That's because snow keeps in the warmth from the ground.

5. Look for signs of life under the drift. You might see green plants or even tunnels made by mice.

INSECTS IN THE COLD

Winter is hard for many animals—including insects. They have to survive cold temperatures, and in many places, there is little food or unfrozen water. Some kinds of insects live on as eggs, which hatch in spring. Some spend winter as young insects, like caterpillars, or wrapped up in hard skins as "pupae." Other insects live as adults by staying in shelters like hives, or hibernating (sleeping) for the winter. And a few migrate. They head for warmer places in the fall, then return in spring. See the chart for some examples of how insects survive winter.

ISABELLA MOTH CATERPILLAR

BUTTERFLY PUPA

GRASSHOPPER EGGS

How They Survive Winter

Insect	Method
Ant	Adults hibernate underground.
Ladybug	Adults hibernate between rocks and under leaves.
Isabella moth	Young live as caterpillars under grass or leaves.
Honeybee	Adults live in hives.
Grasshopper	Eggs live in soil.
Monarch butterfly	Adults migrate to the U.S.A. and Mexico.
Swallowtail butterfly	Pupae live on plant stems or fence posts.
Cricket	Eggs live in the ground.
Mosquito	Some female adults live in logs or houses.
Wasp	Queens hibernate underground or in woodpiles.

MAP THE HIDEAWAYS

Tools

- Notepad and pencil

Steps

1. Make a drawing of your yard to use in this activity.

2. Search carefully for wintering insects. Look under firewood, among rocks, in cracks, among fallen leaves, in thick clumps of grass and weeds, on plants, trunks and twigs, and under loose sidings on sheds.

3. Wherever you discover eggs, young insects, pupae or adults, use an "X" to mark the spots on your drawing.

ROCKS

HOUSE

TREES

FIREWOOD SHED

4. Choose a sunny, warm day to search for hibernating insects that waken for a few hours. Watch for slow-moving beetles, flies and others, especially on the south side of rocks, trees and buildings. Try to flnd their hibernating spots.

5. Check all the places marked on your drawing later—especially in early spring. See if the insects have changed.

FREEZING FACTS

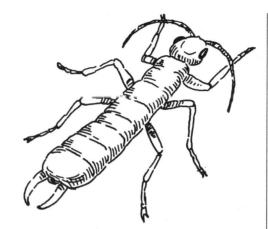

- There is a mountain insect called an "ice worm" that is sometimes found on glaciers.

Warm room temperatures can kill it.

- As pupae, some insects can survive temperatures as low as 58° below 0.
- Honeybees keep moving to stay warm. If the temperature drops to 55° Fahrenheit, they gather in a tight ball and eat honey.

FROM CONES COME GIANTS

Trees are the tallest and oldest living things on Earth. They may be 400 feet tall and hundreds of years old. Trees that produce cones—called coniferous trees—usually live longer than trees that don't produce cones. For centuries, coniferous trees have been providing food and shelter for birds, insects and other animals.

Some people think coniferous trees don't have leaves. But their needles are leaves—special ones that help the tree survive year-round. The needles are covered with wax to prevent drying and filled with sticky material to prevent freezing.

KNOW YOUR CONES

Tools
- Nail file
- Magnifying glass

Steps

1. Pick a cone from a tree. It may be big or small, round or long, depending on the kind of tree. Only cones from pine trees are called "pine cones."

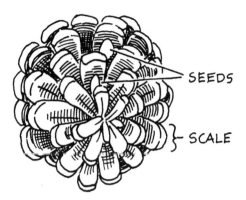

SEEDS

SCALE

2. Look at the way overlapping scales make up the cone. They protect the seeds underneath. When the seeds mature and the weather is right, the scales open or fall off. That lets the seeds out so they can blow or drift to the soil.

3. Use your nail file to pry one of the scales open. Try to spot a seed beneath the scale. If you have a

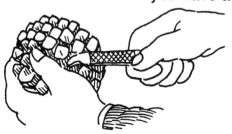

TREE-MENDOUS TREES

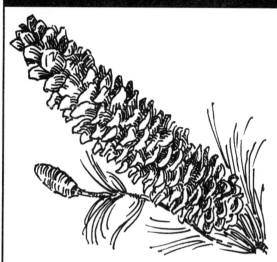

- America's biggest cone: Sugar Pine (up to 5 inches wide and 26 inches long, which is about as long as the pillow on your bed).
- America's smallest cone: One-seed Juniper, ($\frac{1}{8}$ to $\frac{1}{4}$ inch long, which is about as long as the letter "O").

very small cone, use your magnifying glass to look for the seed.

4. Put the cone in your house for a few days. Cones react to changes in heat and moisture. The warmer, drier "weather" in your house may cause the scales on some cones to open a bit.

SIZE A TREE

Tools

- Measuring tape
- Broom

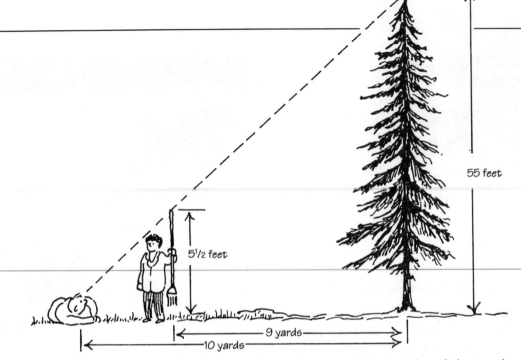

55 feet

5½ feet

9 yards

10 yards

Steps

1. Measure across your yard to a spot 9 yards from a tree. Ask a friend to stand at that spot, holding a broom.

2. Measure 1 yard farther—10 yards from the tree. Kneel at that spot.

3. Put your head close to the ground and look up at the top of the tree. If you were drawing an imaginary line from the top of the tree to yourself, note where it would touch your friend. If the line would be above your friend, ask him or her to raise the broom until the imaginary line would touch the top of the handle.

4. Measure the height of that point on your friend or the broom.

5. Multiply the height by 10 to estimate the height of the tree. For example, the imaginary line may touch the tip of the broom handle 5 ½ feet above the ground. Then the tree would be about 55 feet tall.

TRACKS 'N' TRAILS

It's fun to make tracks in snow or wet mud. When you make a string of them, you leave a trail that others can "read." It tells them something about how big you are and about other things, like whether you were walking or running.

Of course, animals make tracks and trails, too. You can "read" them to discover what kinds of animals have been in your backyard and to guess what they were doing, such as finding food or chasing other animals. But don't be fooled. Things that are not animals also make "tracks": leaves blowing, cones rolling and snow falling off branches.

TELL TALES FROM TRACKS

Tools

- Measuring tape

Steps

1. Check your yard often for tracks. Try to figure out what made them by comparing them with information in the chart on the next page.

- Notice the shape of the tracks, the number of toes and any toenail or claw marks.
- Measure the size of the tracks.

- Measure the width of the trail.
- Compare the pattern of the tracks with those in the chart.

2. Look for other clues.
- A crow often drags its middle toe.

- A mouse sometimes drags its tail.

- A short animal walks under a low branch; a taller one walks around it or steps over it.
- A squirrel's trail usually begins and ends at a tree.

3. Watch for signs of what the animal was doing.
- Notice where the tracks come from and where they are going.

- Check tracks that meet. Look for signs of a chase or a fight, like scrambled snow, feathers or fur.

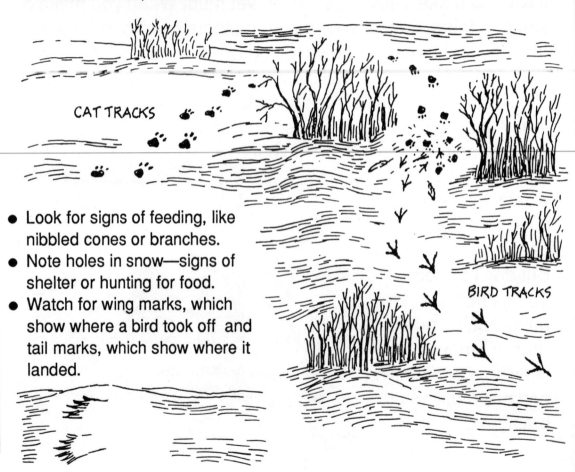

CAT TRACKS

BIRD TRACKS

- Look for signs of feeding, like nibbled cones or branches.
- Note holes in snow—signs of shelter or hunting for food.
- Watch for wing marks, which show where a bird took off and tail marks, which show where it landed.

Animal Tracks and Trails

Animal	Track (inches)		Trail Width (inches)	Track Pattern
Cat	1 x 1	🐾	3	
Dog	Varies	🐾	Varies	
Rabbit	Front: 1 x ³/₄	🐾	4 to 5	
	Back: 3 x 1	🐾		
Squirrel	Front: 1¹/₂ x 1	🐾	3 to 5	
	Back: 2 x 1	🐾		
Mouse	Front: ¹/₄ x ¹/₄	🐾	1¹/₂ to 2	
	Back: ¹/₄ x ¹/₄	🐾		
Crow	Length: 3	🐦	Narrow	
Small bird	Length: 1¹/₂ to 2¹/₂	🐦	Narrow	

FACTS ON TRACKS

- Tracks that look like human footprints, 18 inches long, have appeared in western Canada. Some people think they were made by a sasquatch—a mythical ape-like creature of the woods.
- Diplodocus, one of the longest, four-footed, plant-eating dinosaurs on Earth, left tracks as big as serving trays.

HARD ROCK, SOFT ROCK

At first glance, rocks may not look very interesting. But every rock contains 2 or more of Earth's 1500 minerals—including graphite for pencils, salt for food and gold for jewellery. Some rocks also contain fossils—the remains or shapes of plants and animals that lived on Earth millions of years ago. Layers of mud buried things, like dead fish. Then the mud slowly hardened to stone with the shape of the fish in it.

Rocks are very valuable. They are important sources of building materials, metals and energy. And when they break down, rocks produce soil.

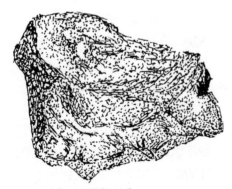

SANDSTONE

CONGLOMERATE

UNCOVER A ROCK

Tools

- Magnifying glass

Steps

1. Find a few rocks in or near your yard. You might have to dig a bit. Choose ones about the size of your fist.

Some Common Rocks

Rock	Color	Feel	Other Features
Sandstone	Most colors, often light brown	Grainy	Some crumble.
Limestone	Mostly gray, cream or pale yellow	Rough or smooth	Some have fossils.
Shale	Mostly gray, dark green, or red brown	Soft and gritty	Some have fossils. Some have thin cracks.
Conglomerate	Mostly sandy colors	Uneven, rough & smooth	Most contain rounded pebbles held together like fruit in a fruit cake.
Granite	Gray, white, or pink with black flakes	Gritty	Most glitter in sunshine.

2. Wash the rocks well to remove all the dirt. Then use a magnifying glass to check for shining minerals.

3. Run your hands over the rocks to see how they feel. Notice the colors in each. Look for any special features, like patterns, streaks, or cracks. Compare your rocks with the common rocks in the chart, but yours may not be described. There are many, many different kinds of rocks.

FORM A ROCK GROUP

Steps

1. See if you can group your rocks using the list below. That is, group them by feel, then by color, and so on. Think of other ways to group your rocks.

- Smooth and rough
- Heavy and light
- Light-colored and dark-colored
- Shiny and dull

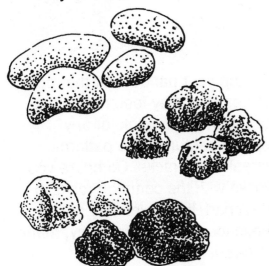

- Solid-colored and multi-colored
- Patterned and plain

2. Choose the group of rocks that you like best and start a collection. When you visit places where you can pick up rocks, you can add to your collection.

SCRATCH AND CRACK

Tools

- Penny
- Metal nail
- Thick rag
- Hammer

Steps

1. Check to see how soft or hard your rocks are. Try to scratch each one with your fingernail, a penny, then a metal nail. Your fingernail will scratch only the softest ones. The penny may scratch some that

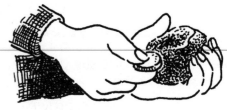

your fingernail can't. The metal nail may scratch harder ones. But some of your rocks may be too hard even for the nail to scratch.

ROCK TALK

- Some dinosaurs swallowed stones to help digest food. Their stomachs polished these stones smooth.
- Rocks are the oldest things on Earth.
- Diamonds are Earth's hardest natural materials.

not hit a rock unless it is wrapped completely. Flying pieces could hurt you.)

2. Wrap a rock several times in a **THICK** rag, like an old towel. Place it on the driveway or sidewalk. Hit the rock in the rag with a hammer. Try other rocks wrapped the same way. Some will crumble. Some will break cleanly. There will be some you cannot break. (**WARNING**: Do

3. Compare the insides with the outsides of rocks that break. See if the color is different. Check for patterns or lines inside the rocks.

JAY DAY

Lots of birds head south for the winter, but check your yard for jays. They're easy to find because they are bright, handsome, and very noisy.

There are different kinds of jays. In the East, the most common ones in backyards are the blue jay; west of the Rocky Mountains the Steller's jay is the most common. These bouncy birds are also common in forests, parks, and campsites. They help spread the seeds of trees and warn other wildlife of danger.

POINT OUT A JAY

Steps

1. Watch to see if jays visit your yard this winter.

2. Notice their size, shape, color, calls, and special features.
- **Size:** about a foot long

- **Blue jay color**
  - bright blue
  - white spots on wings and tails
  - grey-white front
  - blue crest on head

- **Steller's jay color**
  - blue lower back
  - blue wings and tail
  - dark front
  - dark crest on head

- **Tail:** rounded
- **Bill:** stocky and pointed
- **Feet:** 3 toes forward and 1 toe back
- **Call:** loud and varied

3. Watch how the jay moves.
- On the ground, it hops or bounds, but never walks.
- In the air, it flies with deep wing beats.

4. Listen to the jay's calls. Try to hear different ones and notice why the jay changes them. For example, it may shriek when scared. Jay calls include the ones below.

- **Blue jay calls**
  - jay, jay
  - too-wheedle, too-wheedle
  - cla, cla, cla, cla

- **Steller's jay calls**
  - shaak, shaak, shaak
  - klook, klook, klook
  - ca-phee, ca-phee, pheeze-ca

ENJOY A JAY

Tools

- Shallow wood or plastic container
- Bird seed and peanuts
- Water bowl

Steps

1. Attract a jay by making bird noises. Try whistling or noisily kissing your hand. The jay will be curious. It may try to find out what is making the noises.

2. Stay where the jay can see you. Watch while it hunts for food in your yard. Most jays get used to people quickly but remain cautious.

3. Put out bird seed, including sunflower seeds, in a shallow wood or plastic container. Do not use metal containers because small birds might freeze their tongues to the metal. Jays may be a bit shy at first, but they usually come to a feeder. Add a few whole peanuts. (A jay has been seen holding 5 peanuts in its mouth all at once.)

HURRAY FOR THE JAY

- For winter food, blue jays hide acorns on the ground, then forget to eat some. These acorns sprout and grow into oak trees.
- A jay can imitate the cry of a hawk.

REMEMBER: Only start a feeder if you plan to keep it up for the winter. Birds come to depend on you.

4. Provide a bowl of drinking water each day, too. If it freezes, break the ice.

5. Watch how a jay feeds. It often drives other birds from the feeder so it can eat.

INDEX

Diane Swanson enjoys exploring her own backyard—toothy tongues and all—in Victoria, British Columbia. She believes the best way to arouse children's interest in nature is to cultivate their fascination with the common plants and animals near home.

During her writing career, she has produced more than 200 articles—many on outdoor topics—for numerous periodicals, including children's nature magazines such as *Ranger Rick* and *Owl*. She has also written social studies and science books for children in Canadian schools and a host of video scripts, booklets, newsletters, brochures, manuals, and training materials for businesses and university and government departments.